22.95

D1272565

With love to Simon,
the Stringston shark

JUL 1 9 2002

First published in Great Britain in 2002 by Bloomsbury Publishing Plc
38 Soho Square, London, W1D 3HB

Text and illustrations copyright © Jill Newton 2002
The moral right of the author/illustrator has been asserted

All rights reserved
No part of this publication may be reproduced or
transmitted by any means, electronic, mechanical, photocopying
or otherwise, without the prior permission of the publisher

A CIP catalogue record of this book is available from the British Library
ISBN 0 7475 5375 0

Designed by Tracey Cunnell

Printed in Hong Kong by South China Printing Co. Ltd.

1 3 5 7 9 10 8 6 4 2

Bored Claude

Jill Newton

Newmarket Public Library

BLOOMSBURY
CHILDREN'S
BOOKS

I'm SO bored!'
wailed Claude the shark.

'How can you possibly be bored when there's always so much gardening to be done?' called the fish.
Claude yawned.

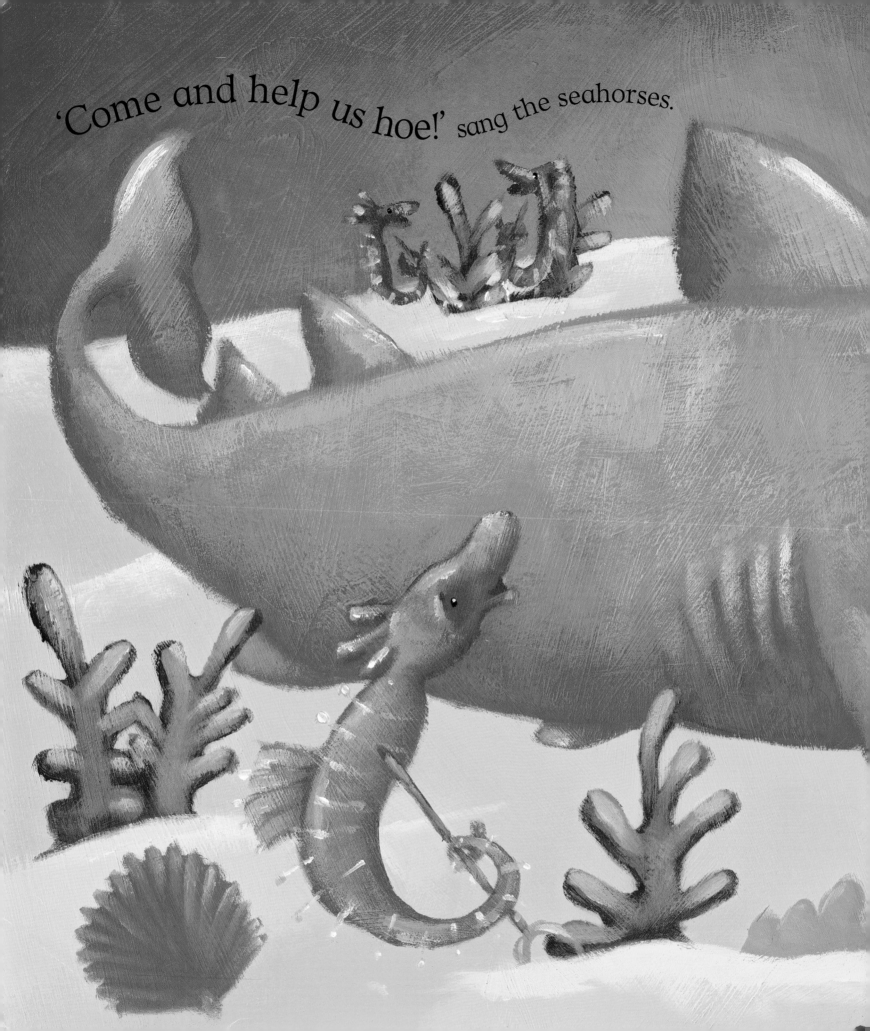

'Come and help us hoe!' sang the seahorses.

Claude swam over to hoe,

but soon lost interest.

'Come and help us prune!' clacked the crabs.

Claude swam over to prune,

but didn't really enjoy it.

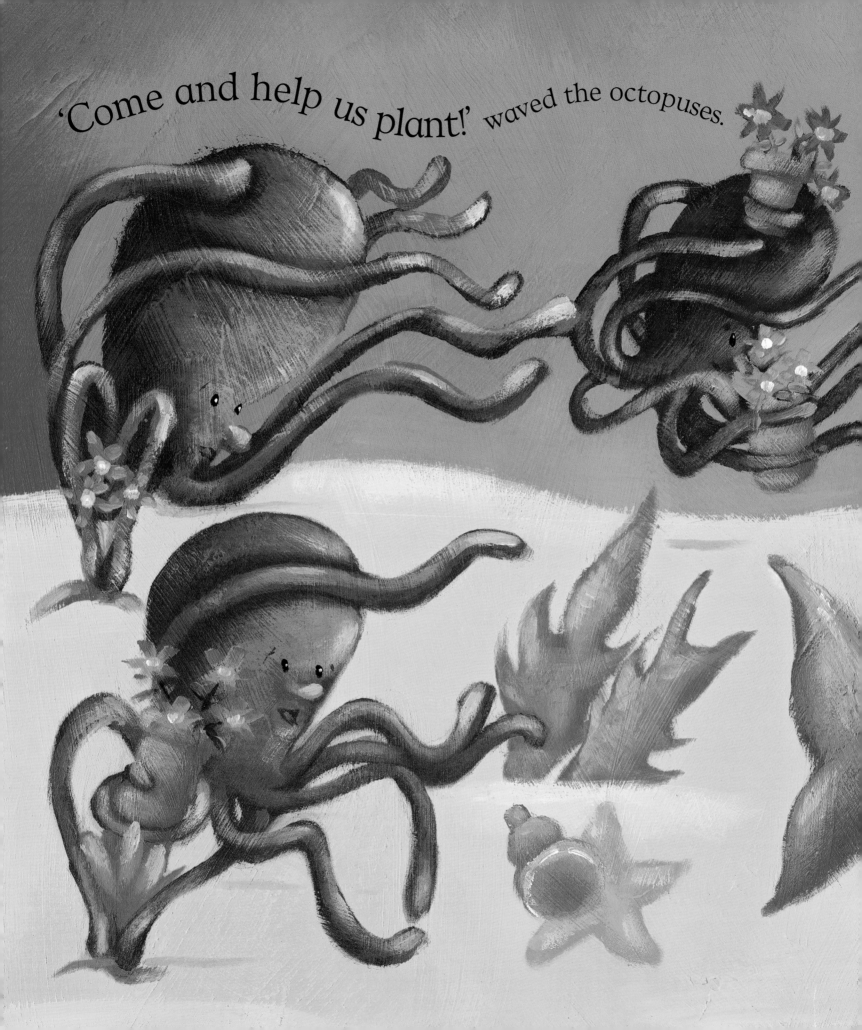

'Come and help us plant!' waved the octopuses.

Claude swam over to plant,

but planting didn't seem his thing.

'Come and water the flowers!' fluttered the angel fish.

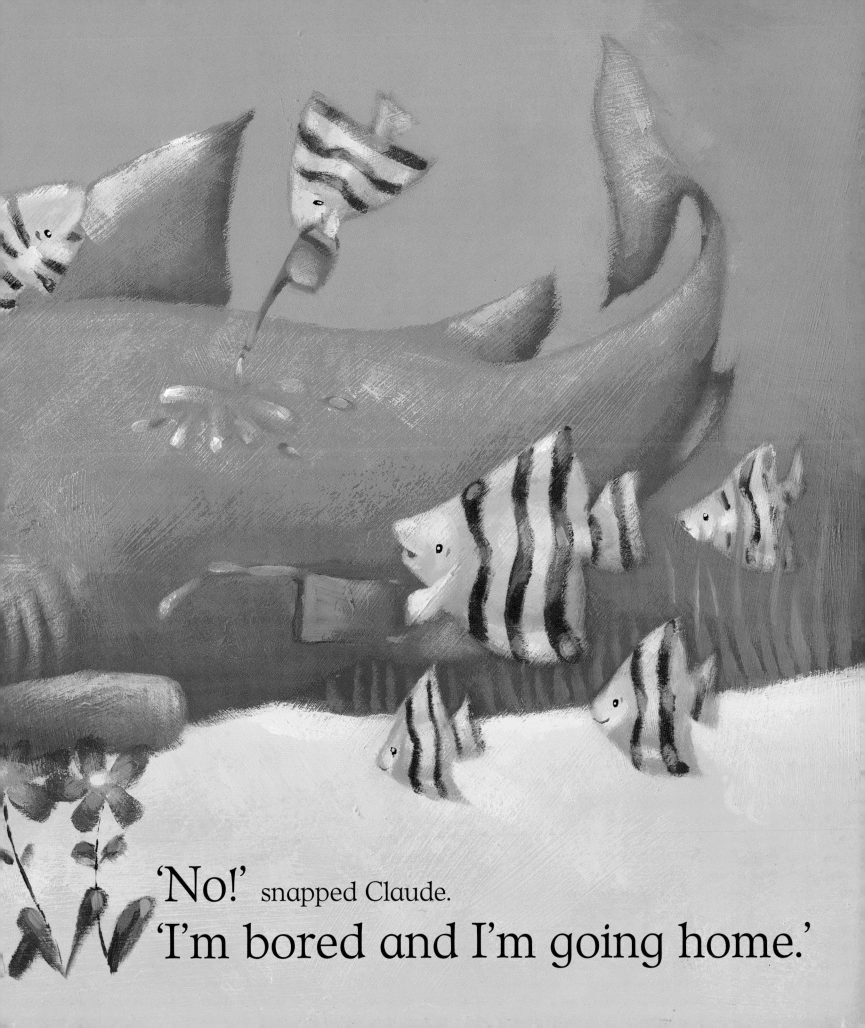

'No!' snapped Claude.
'I'm bored and I'm going home.'

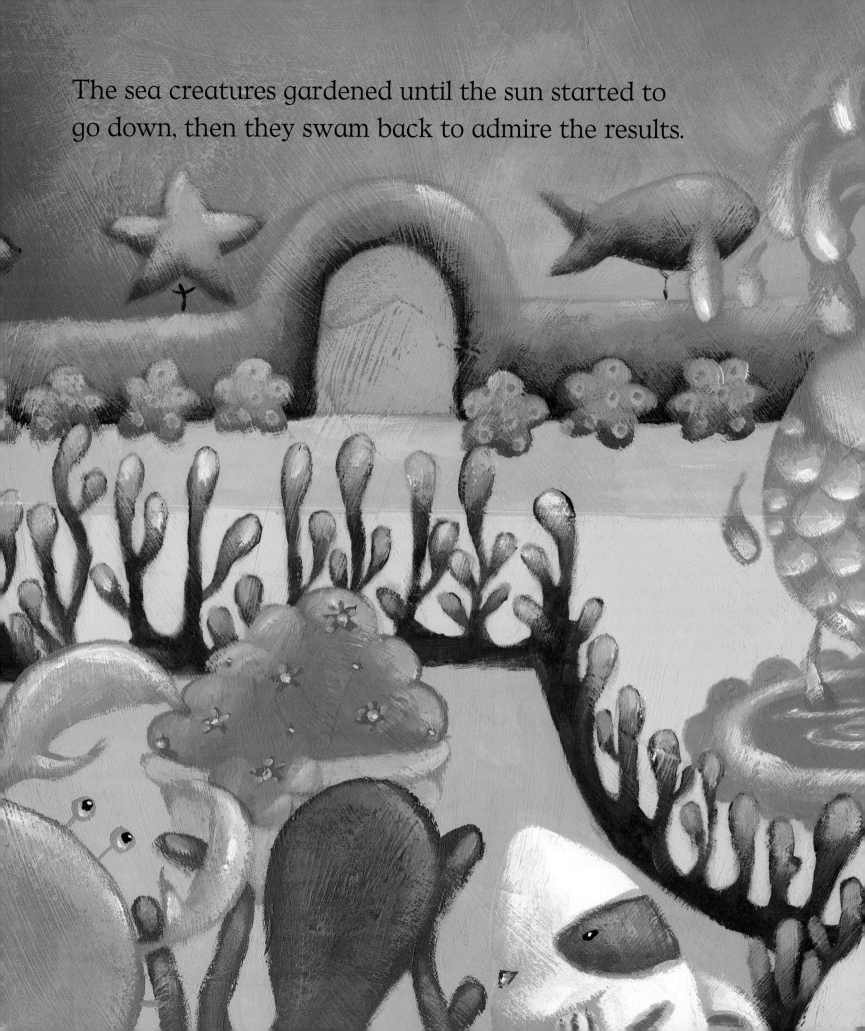

The sea creatures gardened until the sun started to
go down, then they swam back to admire the results.

The garden looked stunning!

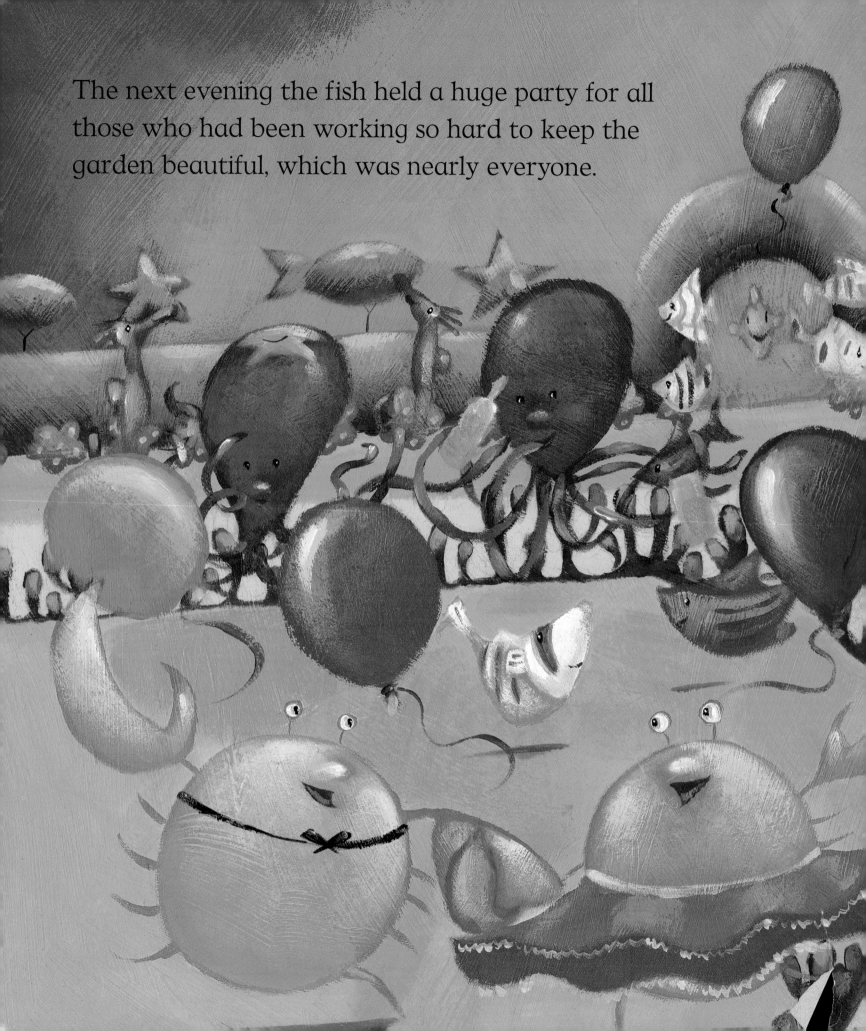

The next evening the fish held a huge party for all those who had been working so hard to keep the garden beautiful, which was nearly everyone.

Claude wasn't invited,

because Claude
hadn't worked hard.

Now Claude was

REALLY

bored.

He heard the singing and laughing
and music and felt sad and lonely.

Then he had a great idea!

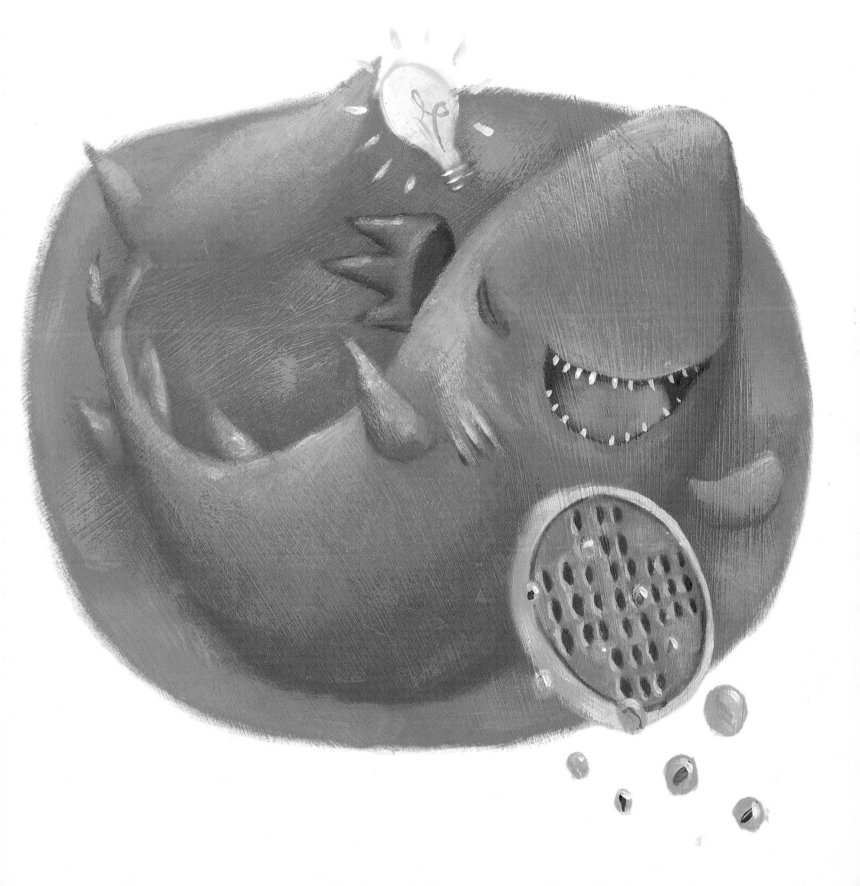

Claude went into his kitchen and started busily

mixing and **stirring** and

rolling and

whisking and

waited . . .

. . . then iced.

When it was finished, Claude swam
to the party with what he had made.

'You made this?' sang the fish.
'But it's the most magnificent cake. It must have taken ages!'
'It was no bother,' said Claude. 'I enjoyed doing it.'

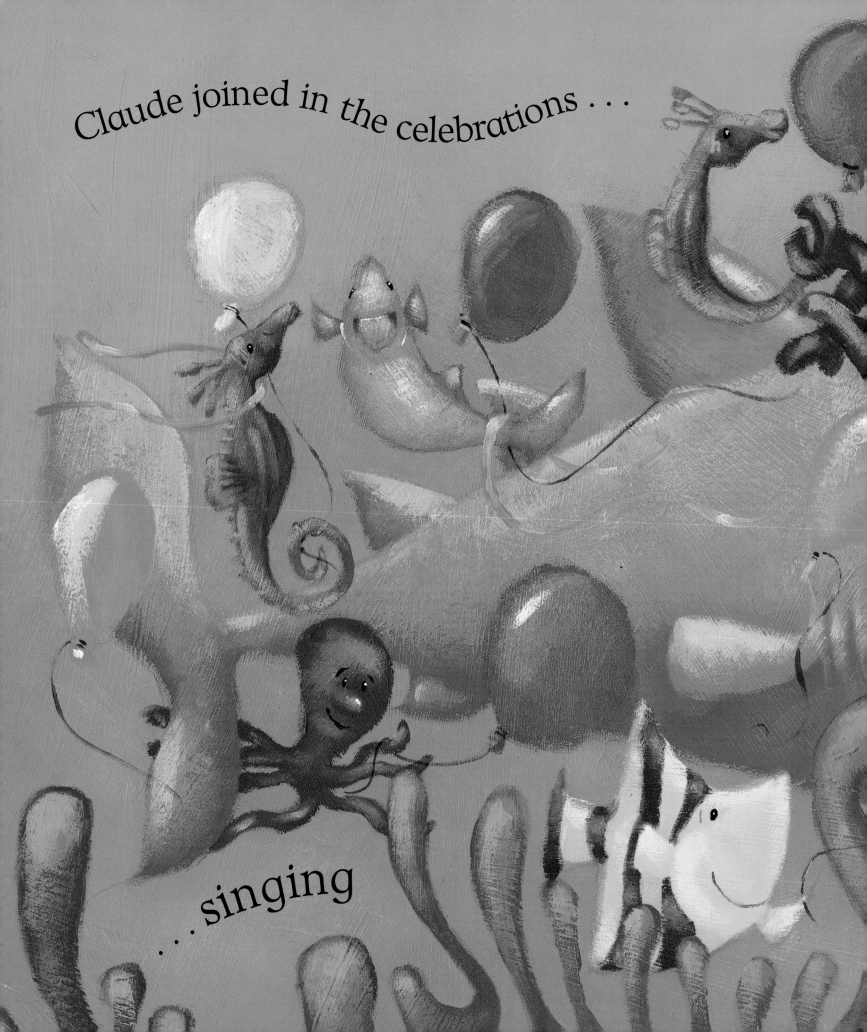

Claude joined in the celebrations . . .

. . . singing

and laughing

and dancing.

The next day when the sea creatures set about
their gardening chores, Claude was around to help.

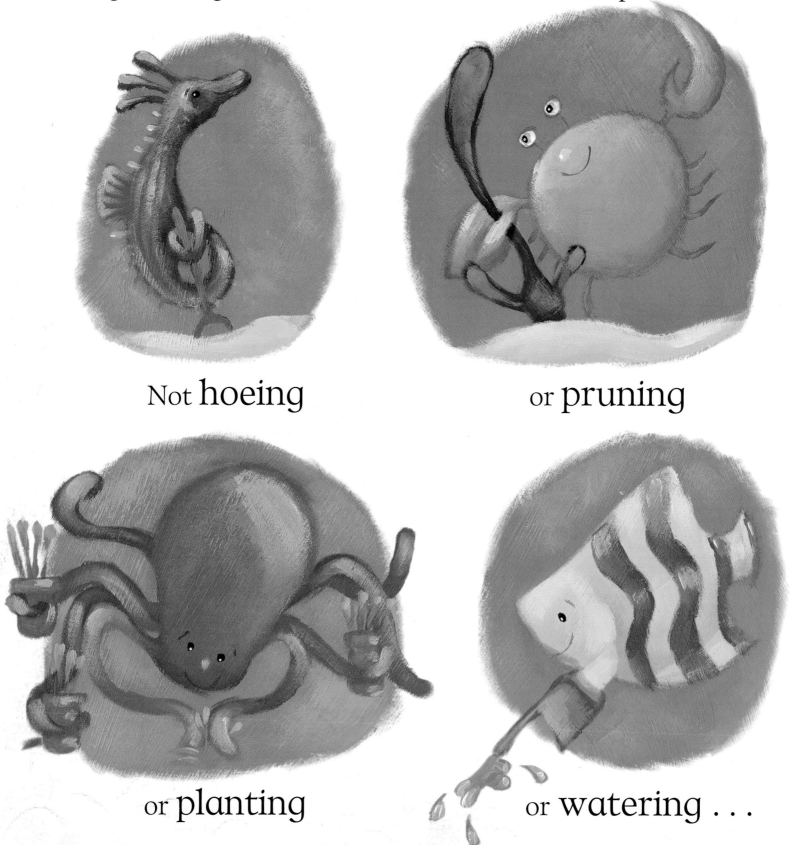

Not hoeing

or pruning

or planting

or watering . . .

. . . but making tea.

Newmarket Public Library